To my little circus piggies, Isabella and Brooklyn.
—S. B-Q.

To my mother, who, like Poppy's mother,
has always encouraged me.
—S. D.

**Library of Congress Cataloging-in-Publication Data Available**

2   4   6   8   10   9   7   5   3

Published by Sterling Publishing Co., Inc.
387 Park Avenue South, New York, NY 10016
Text copyright © 2006 by Sudipta Bardhan-Quallen
Illustrations copyright © 2006 by Sarah Dillard
Distributed in Canada by Sterling Publishing
$c/o$ Canadian Manda Group, 165 Dufferin Street
Toronto, Ontario, Canada M6K 3H6
Distributed in the United Kingdom by GMC Distribution Services,
Castle Place, 166 High Street, Lewes, East Sussex, England BN7 1XU
Distributed in Australia by Capricorn Link (Australia) Pty. Ltd.
P.O. Box 704, Windsor, NSW 2756, Australia

*Printed in China*

Sterling ISBN-13: 978-1-4027-2411-4
ISBN-10: 1-4027-2411-X

For information about custom editions, special sales, premium and
corporate purchases, please contact Sterling Special Sales
Department at 800-805-5489 or specialsales@sterlingpub.com.

# TIGHTROPE POPPY
## the High-Wire Pig

By **Sudipta Bardhan-Quallen**

Illustrated by **Sarah Dillard**

**Sterling Publishing Co., Inc.**

New York

Every day, the pigs would play
and wallow, slow and sloppy.
They rolled in muck
and blessed their luck—
except for one, named Poppy.

Poppy was the kind of pig
who loved big top dramatics:
the clowns in cars,
the juggling stars,
the daring acrobatics.

Of all the things in circus rings
that Poppy did admire,
what made her beam,
her secret dream,
was always the high wire.

So Poppy practiced all the time
on fences and on railings.
She crept along,
she hummed a song,
and never thought of failing.

When Poppy walked to town one day,
she saw a circus flyer:

COME VOLUNTEER!
WE'LL TRAIN YOU HERE
TO WALK ON THE HIGH WIRE.

NEST
BUILDING
SEMINAR

FRIDAY 6:00

BARN
SALE
Saturday
8-4
at
The Barn

COME &
VOLUNTEER!

HAVE YOU
SEEN THIS
LAMB?

last seen
in pasture

She grabbed the flyer and she squealed,
"I'll be a star in no time!"
She headed back
to plan and pack
and told her Mom, "It's show time!"

Then Poppy called farewell to all
and left the farmyard humming.

She twirled her tail
and hit the trail.
"Watch out, big top,
I'm coming!"

A circus dog,
now that is fine.
But have you heard
of circus swine?

At Zig E. Zailey's big top tent
the show was just beginning.
They did, in fact,
need tightrope acts—
"Take me!" said Poppy, grinning.

Though Zig agreed that she'd succeed,
he warned her, "Slow and steady."
But Poppy laughed,
"I know my craft!
I know that I am ready."

Well, Zig just frowned.
He made no sound
as Poppy climbed the spire.

With bursting pride
she took a stride
and stepped out
on the wire.

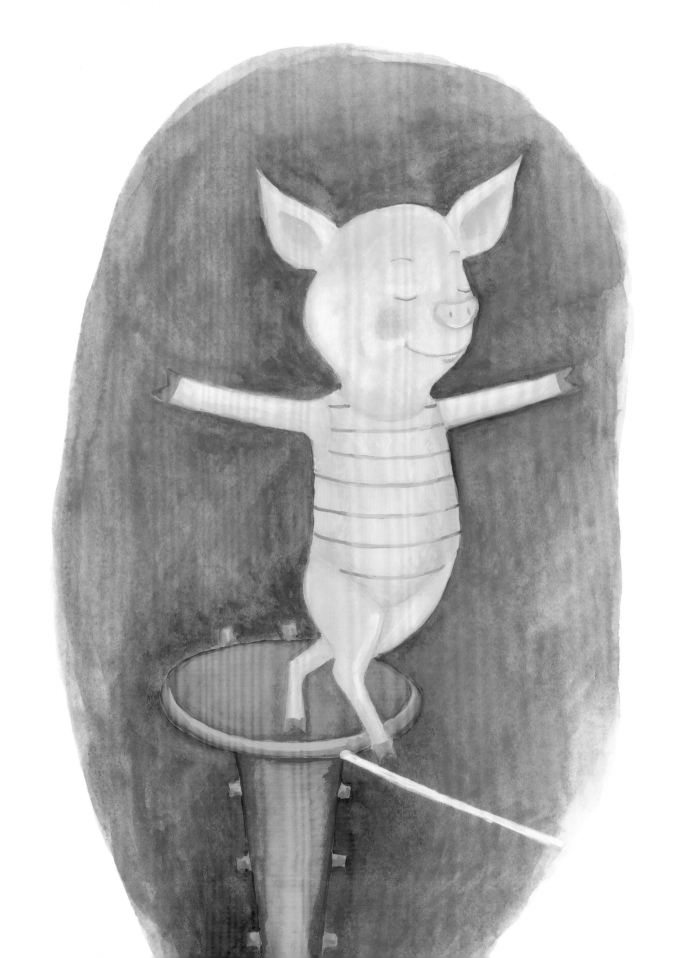

And **PLOP!**

She dropped.

No one spoke or made a joke—
the crowd stood stunned and gaping.
Her face went red
and Poppy fled.
Her thoughts were of escaping.

When Zig proclaimed, "Don't be ashamed!"
Poor Poppy felt no better.
Her pride was bruised
and, all confused,
she e-mailed Mom a letter:

I'm no star. Let's not pretend.
I tried.
I failed.
No more.
The End.

*My dearest Poppy,* Mom replied,
*I know you're sad and crying.*
*You can't lose heart*
*on one bad start—*
*some dreams take lots of trying.*

Poppy read and scratched her head,
and weighed what Mom was saying.
The words felt right.
By late that night,
she knew that she'd be staying.

Poppy walked back to the tent.
Her tummy was still churning.
She raised her snout
and shouted out,
"I'm here to do some learning!"

Balance, focus, straightened spine—
practice makes a tightrope swine.

Zig suggested tippy-toes.
"That might just be the answer."
It started swell,
but when she fell
she landed on a dancer.

She would not quit and, bit by bit,
her footsteps grew more steady.
The weeks, they passed,
until at last
Zig told her she was ready.

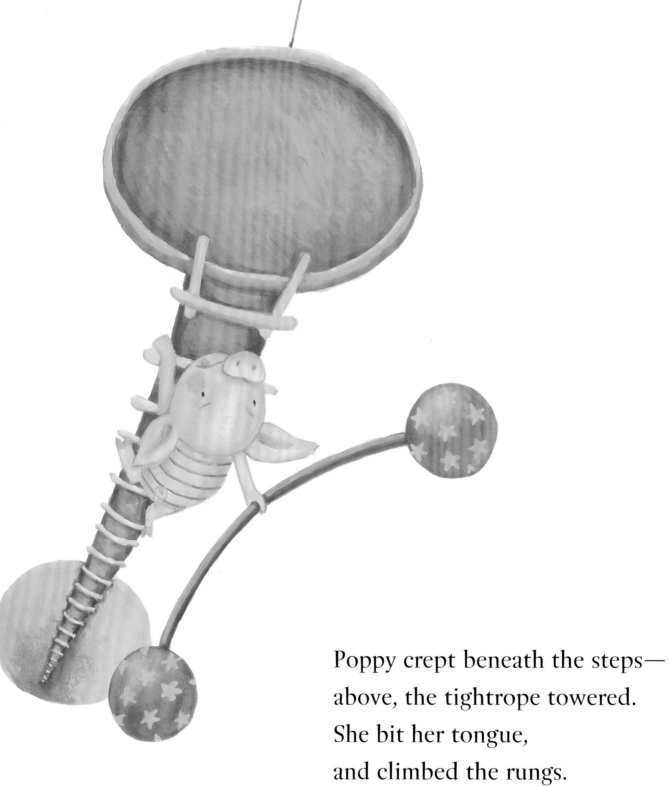

Poppy crept beneath the steps—
above, the tightrope towered.
She bit her tongue,
and climbed the rungs.
She would not be a coward.

She stood up tall, above it all.
She heard her tummy rumble.
Though full of dread,
she inched ahead
until—she took a tumble!

The circus crowd grew still and hushed
when Poppy started flopping.
She hit the net,
and broke a sweat,
but cried, "This time, no stopping!"

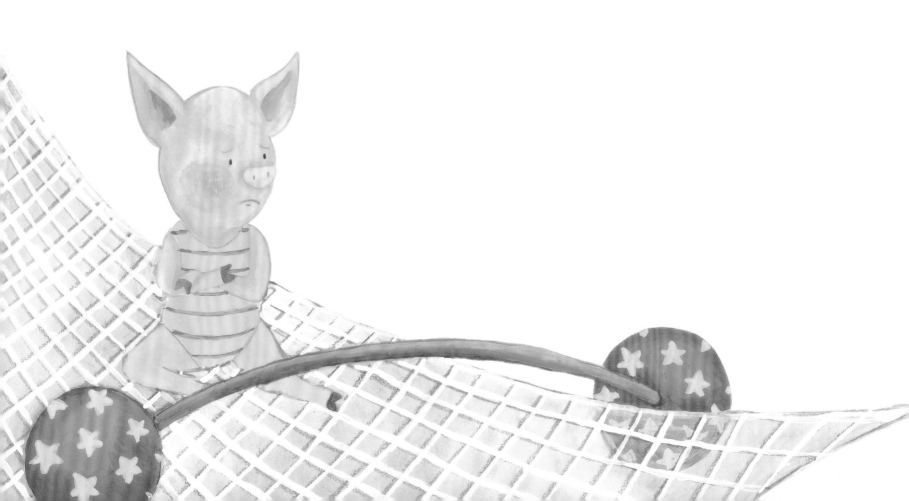

She climbed the spire once again.
Poor Poppy's head was whirling.
She stepped, and stepped,
and stepped,
and stepped,
and then . . .

. . . she started **twirling!**

She launched into a somersault—
she'd never risen higher!
With one last spin,
and one huge grin,
she conquered the high wire!

Then every night, beneath the lights,
she was the main attraction.
Her tightrope skill
gave such a thrill,
she got a huge reaction.

So Poppy wrote another note
to ask her Mom to visit:
*I've reached the heights*
*you said I might.*
*It's never easy, is it?*
*I did not quit! Now I'm a hit.*
*I've sent a brand-new flyer.*

THE STAR of the HIGH WIRE

By Poppy's head
the letters read:

THE STAR OF THE HIGH WIRE.

Come see the show—our star is big!
Her name is Poppy, Tightrope Pig!